For John and Andi

Henry Holt and Company, LLC, *Publishers since 1866*
175 Fifth Avenue, New York, New York 10010 [www.HenryHoltKids.com]

Henry Holt® is a registered trademark of Henry Holt and Company, LLC.
Copyright © 2010 by Doug Cushman
All rights reserved. Distributed in Canada by H. B. Fenn and Company Ltd.

Library of Congress Cataloging-in-Publication Data
Cushman, Doug.
Halloween good night / by Doug Cushman. — 1st ed.   p.   cm.
Summary: On Halloween night, monsters, from hairy werewolves on the moors
to scaly swamp creatures in a black lagoon, say good night to their mommies and daddies.
ISBN 978-0-8050-8928-8
[1. Stories in rhyme. 2. Monsters—Fiction. 3. Bedtime—Fiction. 4. Halloween—Fiction.] I. Title.
PZ8.3.C96Hal 2010   [E]—dc22   2009029428

First Edition—2010 / Designed by Elizabeth Tardiff
Watercolor and ink on Lana watercolor paper were used to create the illustrations for this book.
Printed in March 2010 in China by Macmillan Production (Asia) Ltd., Kwun Tong,
Kowloon, Hong Kong, on acid-free paper. ∞ Supplier Code: 10
1 3 5 7 9 10 8 6 4 2

Halloween Good Night

Doug Cushman

Henry Holt
and Company

New York

When day turns to night with stars overhead,
All Mommas and Papas tuck their kids into bed.
But if you were a monster on Halloween night,
How would you wish your momma and papa **good night?**

If you were a **werewolf** on the moor's muck and mire,
Near an old gypsy cart and a smoldering fire,
With a full yellow moon shining its ghastly moonlight,
How would you tell your hairy papa **good night?**

If you were a **creature** in the dark Black Lagoon,
Snug in your swamp 'neath a watery moon,
Gurgling bubbles as you snuggle in tight,
How would you tell your scaly mommy **good night?**

Glug! Glug!

If you were a **mummy** in a sarcophagus bed,
Wrapped up in linen from your toes to your head,
What would you say in the orange torchlight,
How would you wish your mummy mommy **good night?**

If you were a **skeleton** in a graveyard of stones,
Clacking and rattling all your dry, bleached-out bones,
Yawning a yawn in the ivory moonlight,
How would you tell your bony daddy **good night?**

Clickity-clackity-clack-clack!

If you were a ghost haunting a castle and moat,
Rattling thick chains, making underpants float,
When you stopped all your moaning and screeching in fright,
How would you tell your phantom papa **good night?**

Boo! Boo!

Boo! Boo!

If you were a **witch** with a bubbling brew
Of frog hairs and worm feet and the tongue from a shoe,
When this foul-smelling potion is seasoned just right,
How do you tell your black kitty **good night?**

If you were a **vampire** in your box in the tomb,
As your papa—the Bat—flaps his wings 'round the room
Before he flies off to find someone to bite,
How would you tell your sharp-fanged papa **good night?**

Screeech!

If you were an **alien** in a spaceship from Mars,
Exploring some galaxies, planets, and stars,
Snug in your sleep tube traveling faster than light,
How would you tell your Martian mommy **good night?**

Across the whole world monsters short, thin, and round,
In castles, lagoons, and deep underground . . .

Tuck their kids into bed and pull the blankets up tight.
So how do **you** tell your momma and papa **good night?**

GLOSSARY

ALIEN: ⇧るː۱ːᘓᴥᴥᴥ

BENGALI: শুভরাত্রি
(shubhoratri)

CREATURE: Glug! Glug!

DUTCH: Goede Nacht
(khowdeh nahckt)

FRENCH: Bonne nuit
(bun newee)

GERMAN: Gute Nacht
(gooteh nahckt)

GHOST: Boo! Boo!

GREEK: Καλή νύχτα
(kalinihta)

HEBREW: לילה טוב
(laylah tov)

ITALIAN: Buona notte
(bwona nottay)

JAPANESE: お休みなさい
(o-ya-su-mee-na-sa-ee)

MANDARIN: 晚安 *(wahn ahn)*

MUMMY: 𓏲𓊯𓏏𓇯𓈖

PORTUGUESE: Boa noite
(bohah noytch)

RUSSIAN: Доброй ночи
(dobroy nochi)

SKELETON: Clickity-clackity-clack clack!

SPANISH: Buenas noches
(bwenas nohches)

URDU: شب بخیر
(shub bakhair)

VAMPIRE: Screeeech!

WEREWOLF: Yowwll!

WITCH: Hee! Hee!